# What Will I Be?

*Family life has given me so much.*
*This book is dedicated to the ones I love most. My wife, Judy, who has always been supportive and my children, Josh and Jessica, who continue to inspire me both as an Artist and as a Father.*

*Special thanks to Sam Sommer for all his creative input and long hours and to Sheba Saphow for her creative needle and thread.*

*—J.L.*

*Photography and Concept: James Levin*
*Set Design and Construction: Sam Sommer*

Text copyright © 2001 by Scholastic Inc.
Photographs copyright © 2001 by James Levin.
All rights reserved. Published by Scholastic Inc.
SCHOLASTIC, CARTWHEEL BOOKS and associated logos
are trademarks and/or registered trademarks of Scholastic Inc.

Library of Congress Cataloging-in-Publication Data available

ISBN 0-439-24023-9

12  11  10  9  8  7  6  5  4  3  2  1          01  02  03  04  05

# What Will I Be?

Photographs by James Levin ★ Written by Wendy Lewison

SCHOLASTIC INC.  Cartwheel BOOKS ®

New York  Toronto  London  Auckland  Sydney
Mexico City  New Delhi  Hong Kong

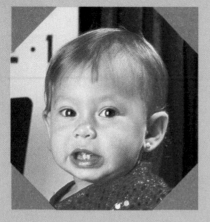

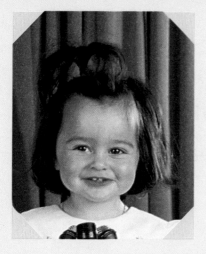

When I grow up, What Will I Be?
Come play a guessing game with me!
You'll find a lot of little clues
to help you name the job I'll choose.

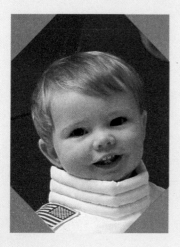

Every morning I will make
bread and bagels, pies and cake,
doughnuts round, and muffins sweet.
Doing my job will be a treat!

# What Will I Be?

A baker.

I'll work with actors every day,

rehearsing to put on a play.

They'll learn their parts and all the rest.

I'll help them be their very best.

# What Will I Be?

A director.

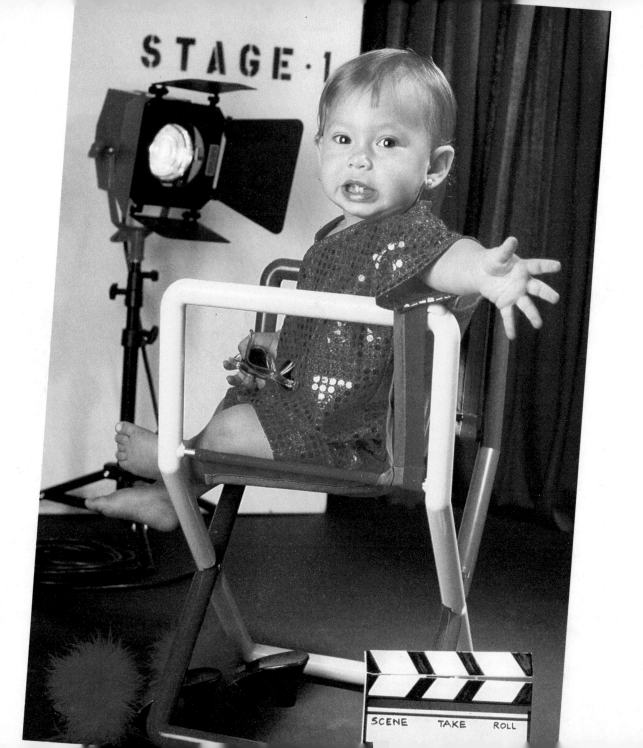

STAGE · 1

SCENE    TAKE    ROLL

My classroom will
be lots of fun.
I'll have a smile
for everyone.
I'll teach my
students things
I know and try
to help them
learn and grow.

## What Will I Be?

A teacher.

I'll wear a badge
that's shiny bright,
and I'll protect you
day and night.
At home, at school,
and all around,
I'll work to keep
you safe and sound.

# What Will I Be?

A police officer.

Point and click
and press that key!
Got a question?
Just ask me.
I love computers
and what they do —
I'll be happy to
answer you!

# What Will I Be?

A computer scientist.

"Yes, Your Honor," is what they'll say
in my courtroom every day.
I'll wear a robe that's very long,
and I'll decide what's right and wrong.

# What Will I Be?

A judge.

Sound the siren, loud and clear.

I've got my hose, my hat, my gear.

I'll be ready — have no doubt.

I'll come to put the fire out!

# What Will I Be?

A firefighter.

I'll have everything it takes
to change those tires and fix those brakes.
"Come to my garage," I'll say.
"You will soon be on your way!"

## What Will I Be?

A mechanic.

In my work clothes, boots, and hat,

I will build things, just like that!

Maybe a bridge for trucks and cars.

Maybe a skyscraper up to the stars!

**What Will I Be?**

A construction worker.

If you want to talk to me,
outer space is where I'll be.
In my spaceship I'll explore
places never seen before.

# What Will I Be?

An astronaut.

I'll point my toes, I'll bend and sway,
I'll leap and twirl the time away.
And then I'll bow quite gracefully
while everybody claps for me.

# What Will I Be?

A dancer.

When you feel sick,
you'll come to me.
I'll check your heart,
I'll tap your knee.
I'll give you medicine
with a spoon,
and you'll feel better
very soon!

## What Will I Be?

A doctor.

I will fly my little plane
into the clouds and out again.
I'll whiz through the air and zoom all around,
then I'll land it safely on the ground.

# What Will I Be?

A pilot.

I'll have an office of my own,
a great big desk, a telephone.
I'll be as busy as can be,
working for my company.

# What Will I Be?

A business person.

Rain and sleet and even snow—
will they stop me? No, no, no!
I'll deliver, I'll get through.
Here's a letter just for you!

# What Will I Be?
A mail carrier.

On TV, I'll give reports

on traffic and weather, business and sports.

I'll cover it all, from A to Z.

If something happens — it's news to me!

## What Will I Be?

A newscaster.

"Smile!" I'll say. "Hold that pose!"

*Snap!* is how the shutter goes.

My camera's ready, the film is in it.

You'll have your picture in a minute!

# What Will I Be?

A photographer.

All the people
will vote for me,
so in the White House
I will be.
I'll lead the country
well, and then
I hope they'll vote
for me again!

## What Will I Be?
The President.